Goodnight,

My Duckling

NANCY TAFURI

DUCK POND PRESS • CONNECTICUT

Sweet dreams to every little duckling —
and to *my* duckling Cristina.

Copyright @ 2005 by Nancy Tafuri.
Originally Published by Scholastic Press
All rights reserved. Now Published by DUCK POND PRESS., Publishers since 2005.
DUCK POND PRESS and its associated logo is a registered trademark.
No part of this book may be reproduced or utilized in any form or by any means,
electronic or mechanical, including photocopying, recording, or by any information
storage and retrieval system, without permission in writing from the Publisher,
DUCK POND PRESS, located at PO Box 168, Roxbury, Connecticut 06783.
www .ttafuri@earthlink.net

LIBRARY OF CONGRESS CATALOGING-IN-PUBLICATION DATA
Tafuri, Nancy
ISBN 978-0-9763369-4-5

Summary: As a mother duck leads her ducklings home, one dawdles and is left
behind but, luckily a friend is there to help the little duckling back to his nest
in time for bed.

DUCK POND PRESS first edition published in 2013
10 9 8 7 6 5 4 3 2 1

Printed in Malaysia

The illustrations were painted in watercolors and inks.

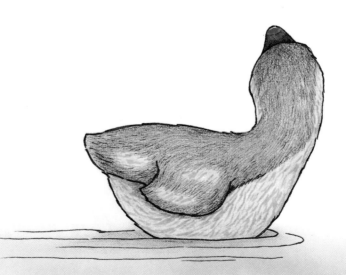

Early one evening . . .

"Time for bed, my ducklings!"

"Goodnight, little duckling."

"Sleep tight,
little duckling."

"See you in the morning, little duckling."

"Hurry home, little duckling."

"Are you lost, little duckling?"

"There you are,
my duckling!"

"Sweet dreams,
little duckling."

"I love you, my duckling."

Goodnight.